STO

FRIENDS
OF ACPL

3 1833 02104 695

W9-CNG-188

jE
Be
The Enchanted closet

THE ENCHANTED CLOSET

BY BETA

THE LION PRESS
NEW YORK

80 586 1

192

Copyright © 1967 by KDI-Lion Press, Inc.
52 Park Avenue, New York, N.Y. 10016
All rights reserved
Published simultaneously in Canada by George J. McLeod, Ltd.
73 Bathurst Street, Toronto 2B, Ontario
ISBN: 0-87460-022-7; Lib. ed: 0-87460-117-7
Library of Congress Catalog Card Number: 67-18483
This book was printed and bound in the United States of America

1756151

THE ENCHANTED CLOSET

Every day at half past four
I open up a closet door.

This is what I always say,
"What will I become today?"

MONDAY

Of all the things that I might be
I wish a BUTTERFLY
Were me.

And so I find a certain box
That has a skirt with polka dots.

I stretch my arms inside its waist
And a BUTTERFLY
I am at last!

TUESDAY

Of all the things that I might be
I wish a GREAT WHITE WHALE
Were me.

I find a pillow soft and white
And Christmas candy round and bright.

With candy as my water spout,
A
GREAT WHITE WHALE
I am at last!

WEDNESDAY

Of all the things that I might be
I wish a DARK HOOT OWL
Were me.

Here are glasses with thick rims,
And two umbrellas tall and slim.

See my wings? I hold them fast,
And a **DARK HOOT OWL**
I am at last!

THURSDAY

Of all the things that I might be
I wish a TURTLE
To be me.

Behind a basket that I found
Some Spanish castanets fall down.

They make a noisy clack-click-clack
And a TURTLE
I become at last!

FRIDAY

Of all the things that I might be
I wish a RABBIT
To be me.

Mama's shoes have pointed toes,
Her furry cape is white as snow.

Cape and shoes are all I ask
And a RABBIT
I become at last!

SATURDAY

Of all the things that I might be
I wish a SPIDER
To be me.

Daddy's shoes and a knitted shawl
Come in handy after all.

(The shoes, you see, are flies I've trapped)

and a SPIDER

I become at last!

SUNDAY

Of all the things that I might be
I wish a **TREE IN SPRING**
Were me.

Among my gloves and Mama's hats
I find one flat potato sack.

I wear them all and stand up straight
And a TREE IN SPRING
I am at last!

At half past five I close the door
And I become myself once more.

No whales, no owls, and no more trees,
Until tomorrow I'll be